UNICORSE

Mum crawls on to the couch for a rest after tucking Bluey into bed for the third time.
"OK, she's finally asleep," Mum says.
"What do you want to watch tonight, babe?" asks Dad.

LADYBIRD BOOKS

UK | USA | Canada | Ireland | Australia | India | New Zealand | South Africa

Ladybird Books is part of the Penguin Random House group of companies
whose addresses can be found at global.penguinrandomhouse.com.

www.penguin.co.uk   www.puffin.co.uk   www.ladybird.co.uk

First published in Australia by Puffin Books 2023
This edition published in Great Britain by Ladybird Books Ltd 2023
001

Text and illustrations copyright © Ludo Studio Pty Ltd 2023

Printed in Italy

The authorized representative in the EEA is Penguin Random House Ireland,
Morrison Chambers, 32 Nassau Street, Dublin D02 YH68

A CIP catalogue record for this book is available from the British Library

ISBN: 978-0-241-64943-5

All correspondence to:
Ladybird Books, Penguin Random House Children's
One Embassy Gardens, 8 Viaduct Gardens, London SW11 7BW

"Do you watch TV after we go to sleep?" interrupts Bluey.

"Bluey!" Mum is getting a bit frustrated. "Back to bed!" But Bluey's having trouble getting to sleep tonight. "Why do we have to sleep? Why can't we just stay awake all night?" she says. "Cos that's the way the world is, kid," answers Dad.

WELL, I'LL TAKE ALL THE COUCHES TO THE DUMP, TOO!

SOUNDS LIKE A BIG JOB. YOU'LL NEED A FULL NIGHT'S SLEEP FOR THAT.

YEAH, I WILL. NIGHT!

HEY, WAIT! NO!

Mum is tired, but she agrees to read Bluey a book.
She wishes Bluey was easier to put to sleep.
"You know she can't help it," says Dad.
"I know. Can you help me?" says Mum.

"Yeah, I have an idea," answers Dad, rushing off.
"Wait, is it a bad idea?" asks Mum.

Bluey climbs on to the couch beside Mum. "Are you grumpy with me?"

"No, honey. I just want you to go to sleep," says Mum. She opens the book and begins to read . . .

Once upon a time, there was a village.
And in the village, everyone walked around barefoot.

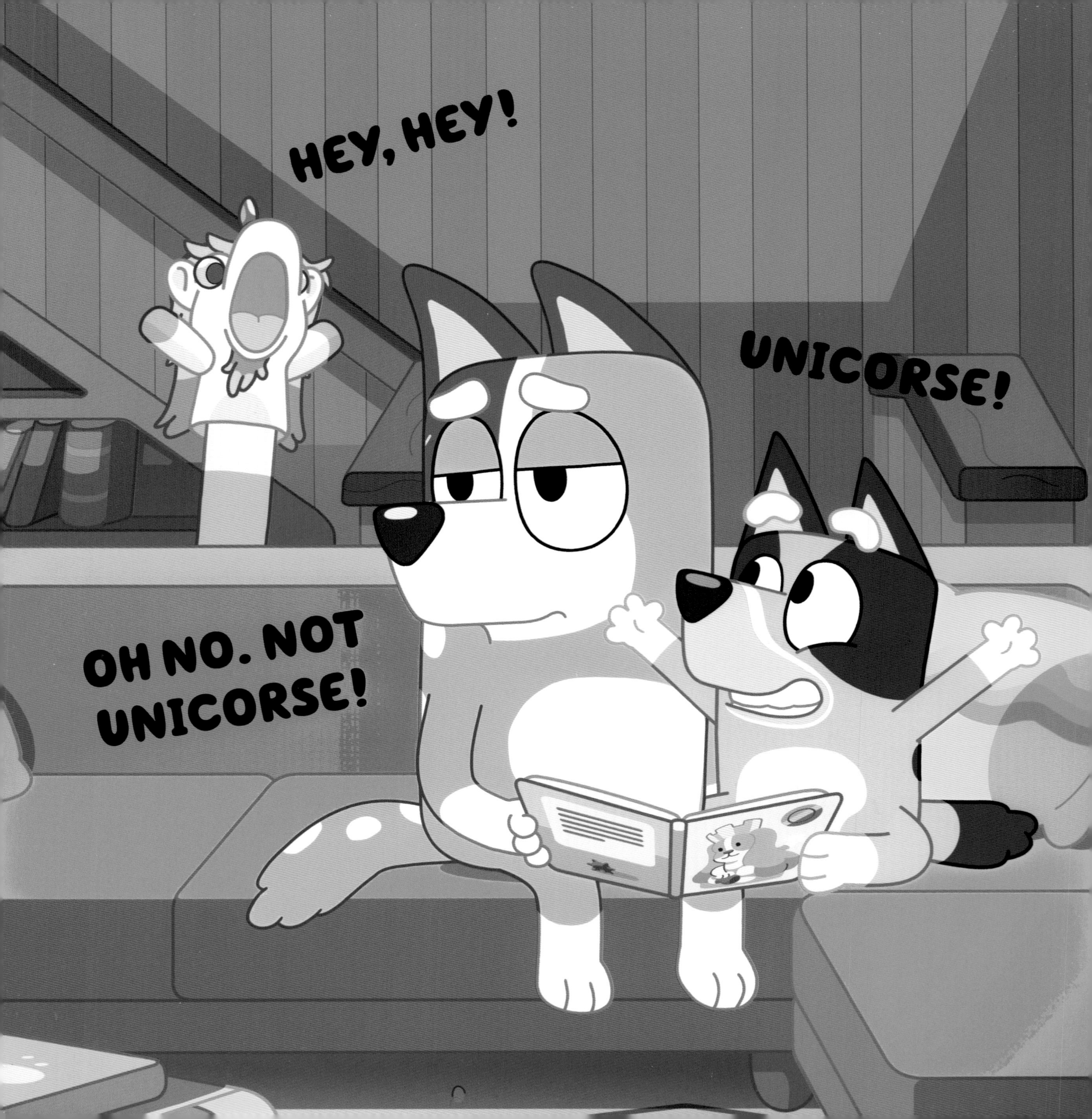
HEY, HEY!
UNICORSE!
OH NO. NOT UNICORSE!

"How about you and your *little mate* jog on," suggests Mum.

I'M NOT GOING ANYWHERE, BILLY.

HEHE!

MY NAME IS CHILLI.

OH, I'M SORRY, SILLY.

THAT'S IT. OUT!!!

OH, MUM, PLEASE CAN UNICORSE STAY?

BLUEY, HE'S THE MOST ANNOYING UNICORSE IN THE WORLD.

GUILTY . . .

BUT I CAN TURN HIM INTO A NICE UNICORSE. I PROMISE.

FINE. HE CAN STAY. BUT WE'RE READING *THIS* BOOK, NOT YOURS.

YOU WILL LIVE TO REGRET THAT!

Mum ignores Unicorse. "Ahem." She reads on, "Once upon a time, there was a village. And in the village, everyone walked around barefoot."

UNICORSE! I CAN'T SEE THE PAGE.

AAAAND . . . WHY SHOULD I CARE?

UGH. I FORGOT ABOUT UNICORSE'S CATCHPHRASE.

IF YOU BLOCK THE WORDS, MUM CAN'T READ THE STORY.

AAAAND . . . WHY SHOULD I CARE?

BECAUSE STORIES ARE NICE.

MY STORY WAS NICE. IT HAD A UNICORN IN IT.

THIS STORY HAS A BORING ENDING. THE QUEEN JUST MAKES SH—

UNICORSE!

HAAAAAA!

Bluey is not having much luck **CHANGING** him. Mum reads on, but Unicorse keeps taking over the story.

MY TURN!

UP . . . DOWN . . . UP . . . DOWN.

UNICORSE, THAT IS BAD BEHAVIOUR.

MEEP, MEEP, MEEP.

SHALL WE CONTINUE?

ERGH, YES.

One day, the Queen decided to get off her litter and have a walk around.

Ouch!

So the Queen walked a few steps, and stood on a prickle.

HA-HA-HAAAAA!

UNICORSE, THAT'S MEAN. HOW WOULD YOU FEEL IF YOU STOOD ON A PRICKLE?

I'D FEEL GOOD. I'D FEEL SO GOOD I WOULD DANCE.

YOU WOULDN'T DANCE. YOU'D BE CRYING, LIKE THE QUEEN.

WELL, MAYBE SHE SHOULD MAKE SOME SHOOOOESSS!

ANYWAY . . .

The Queen discovered that her whole kingdom was covered in prickles.

What was she to do?

So the Queen had an idea.

She will cover the WHOLE kingdom in LEATHER. That way, no one will ever stand on the prickles again.

LOOK, BLUEY. GOOD ON YOU FOR TRYING, BUT YOU CAN'T CHANGE UNICORSE.

ERGH, I THINK YOU'RE RIGHT.

I'M NOT SURE YOU CAN CHANGE ANYONE VERY MUCH.

BUT WHAT CAN WE CHANGE?

WELL, WE CAN STOP LETTING UNICORSE ANNOY US.

REALLY? HOW?

The Queen just couldn't do any more. She was too tired.

But then the Jester said to the Queen, "Your Majesty, instead of covering your whole kingdom in leather...

why not just cover your feet?"

So the Queen cut two little bits of leather...

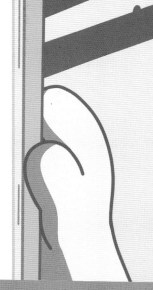

STOP THAT READING. THIS IS A VERY SERIOUS MATTER.

ONE OF YOU KARATE CHOPPED MY CLIENT.

KARATE CHOPPED?!

BLUEY, IGNORE HIM.

OH YEAH, SORRY.

...and made them into shoes!

HEY, I'M TALKING TO YOU.

YEAH. LISTEN TO HIM!

Now the people could walk anywhere they wanted and the prickles couldn't hurt them.

And they all lived happily ever after.

Bluey yawns. Trying to change Unicorse is tiring.

"Shall we leave them to it?" says Mum with a smile.
"Yeah, I'm sleepy," says Bluey, and she heads off to bed.